INCIDENT AT DIAMOND SPRINGS

Kendall Hanson

ISBN: 1-929516-32-0

ISBN-13: 978-1-929516-32-2

Kendall Hanson; Dixon-Price Publishing. Kingston, Washington.

C3

A Quick Note about Stagecoaches

For their day, stagecoaches were somewhat amazing. Few people in the 21st Century realize that coaches on established routes often traveled 24 hours a day. To do that, however, required relay stations where teams could be changed quickly, and for routes where speed was considered essential, the stations might be as little as fifteen miles apart. But under those conditions, stagecoaches could often cover ground twice as fast as "express" riders.

It you are going that fast in a stagecoach, though, you are going to be bumped and bustled every minute of the ride, and as a passenger, you hope the driver is experienced. So many things can go wrong so quickly, not least of which is attack by outlaws or others.

Like gasoline in modern engines, the most important element for a stagecoach was a team of horses. For lines that could afford it, six horses was considered a minimum, but a team of four was often what a smaller line would have.

According to expert driver Doug Hansen, a six-horse team could be compared to a football team. The positions are wheeler, swing, and lead. Wheel horses are the linemen, heavily muscled and durable. They're connected to the pole of the coach, so they must have mass and pulling strength. The swing team are like fullbacks and tight ends: they must have balance and control as well as strength. The lead horses are like quarterbacks and must have confidence and courage to drive into the raging torrent of a river or up a steep, questionable hill.

One of the oddities of the driving profession, though, was how the team rows were referred to. "Near" horses—the near lead, the near swing, the near wheel—were to the left of the driver and actually the furthest from him. The "off" lead, swing, and wheel horses were to his right and thus nearer, generally, than the "near" horses.

And now you know enough to get to the story.

Happy reading!

For Rob.

Contents

CHAPTER ONE

Doubt

The stagecoach had just topped the peak of 10-Mile Hill when Barney Todd noticed a plume of smoke from the southwest in the direction of Diamond Springs.

He elbowed the new shotgun messenger beside him. "What do you think of that, Willy?" Barney said as he nodded toward the distance column of black.

"Is that smoke?" Willy asked.

"What the hell else do you think it would be?" Barney snapped. He wasn't sure of Willy. The young man had been thrust on him just this morning after his regular shotgun Jack Harris had gotten himself cut up in a knife fight at one of Council Grove's less welcoming saloons. If Barney was right, this was Willy's first trip as a shotgun messenger, but the line was required to have one whenever there was a strongbox on board.

Too bad Jack had gotten himself cut up in a foolish barroom brawl. Jack always kept a good look out when he was in the shotgun seat. Willy just seem to look around, not really looking to keep everyone safe.

The smoke on the horizon was bothersome. Barney chance to look over his shoulder at Sun, the Chinaman who always accompanied him on a run. Sun was looking at the smoke as well. He looked at Barney and said, "Big fire."

"Diamond Springs Station?" Sun nodded agreement.

"You really think so?" Willy asked.

"Almost sure of it," Barney replied. "What else would make so much smoke? Best keep a good lookout Willy. We might be having visitors we don''t want."

"I heard that some of Quantrill's Raiders were in the area," Willy said.

"Says who?"

"Burrell at the livery stable told me. Said some farmer had seen them ride by a little south of Council Grove."

Barney shook his head. "Nobody said anything to me."

“Burrell said it was some of the Campey boys.”

“Burrell isn’t always the sharpest spike on the track.” Barney looked down at his team. Since the coach was under – occupied, he only had a team of four horses. The off lead horse was a veteran, but Barney worried about the near lead, a younger gelding that was fast and strong, but a bit skittish. He wasn’t sure that he could depend on him if they had to make a run for it. Barney always felt his first duty was to protect the passengers. The company felt it was to protect the cargo. Usually, he could do both.

“If he’s right, it doesn’t matter if these dumb,” Willy said. ““I don’t mind facing a couple of everyday robbers, but facing the Campey boys is a different matter.”

“If they want the strong box they can have it,” Barney said. “I just wonder if that smoke has anything to do with them. That’’s a pretty big column of smoke.”

“Maybe we should turn around. Just in case.”

“If I turned back every time something might happen I’d never get anywhere. Besides, we are already past the halfway point and there is no place to turn around for another mile or so." Even so, Barney thought to himself, Willy might have a point. But if the Campey brothers had attacked the way station, the people there might need help.

On the other hand, going back to Council Grove would be a long pull for the team. Since they only had three passengers, the station agent had loaded the boot with dry goods for Marion station. The coach was almost as heavy as if it carried of full load of passengers.

Willy shook his head. "I guess you're right. If the Campey brothers attacked the station people might be hurt. Can't imagine why there would be so much smoke else."

"Just keep your eyes open." Barney wondered just how good Willy would be in a firefight. Willy couldn't be more than twenty years old, but he was a good head taller than Barney and certainly wider. "How come you haven't been pulled into the Army? Seems like every young man is being drafted by one side or the other."

"Got a bum leg," Willy said. "Broke it when I fell off my daddy's wagon. About five years ago. Didn't heal up right. I can shoot well enough, but I can't walk very far or run. Tried to enlist for the Union, but they didn't want me. The Confederacy ain't gonna win anyways."

"Sitting down suits you."

"Well, it's pretty sitting up here in the sunshine and looking all around at the grass and the hills." Willy looked all around and waved in front of him. ""I guess you love it too since you've been doing it for so long."

"Sitting down suits me. But it wears out my butt. Don't know how much longer I can do this. It takes its toll on you. But I can't imagine doing anything else.""

"You always bring the Chinaman with you?"

"Last five years. Never asked him. Saved his life outside of Lawrence and now I can't get rid of him." Wouldn't want to, Barney thought to himself. Sun Qi had become his closest friend over the years. He had discovered the Chinaman was a thoughtful man who was tough as nails and probably smarter than Barney.

When Barney had rescued him from a band of drunken yahoos that were beating him for sport as much as anger, Sun Qi determined in his own way that he owed a debt to Barney and would be dishonored if he didn't fulfill it. By now, though, Barney thought of him as his partner, but he could tell that Willy thought he was a servant.

"How much farther to that turn around? Or we're going to turn back or go ahead?"

"Not far. But look over there, off to the left. Tell me what you see."

"Some kind of riders. Think it could be the Campey boys?"

"Could be. Don't look right somehow." As far as Barney could see the riders were spread out, not like a group of militia or bandits would likely be. ""I think it might be Cheyenne."

"What are they doing way out here?" Willy looked confused. "The reservation is way to the south of here."

"Might be a hunting party that's decided to go renegade. I've heard the game has become scarce on the reservation."

"Are they likely to bother us?"

"Guess we'll just have to find out. They're a long ways off. At least three or four miles, I'd say. It's only five more miles to Diamond Springs, and they are between us and the station. You ever shot anyone before?"

"Naw, but it's just a stranger. Can't be much different than hunting and I've done a passel of that."

"No, it's different when someone's shooting at you. Let's hope this is just a hunting party and not a bunch of braves who need to show their manhood. But you're right, I think we might need to turn around just to be on the safe side."

CHAPTER TWO

Dedication

Barney was about to turn his off lead slightly to the right to give the stage room to make a wide turnaround when a small figure jumped into the road ahead about a hundred yards away. The boy was waving his arms and jumping up and down. Barney told Willy to apply the brake slowly and he pulled back on the reins until the stage came to a stop.

The boy was running toward them. He looked about ten, but his face was blackened with soot and he was barefoot, so Barney wasn't sure. "You got to help us!" he was screaming. "My Ma's hurt real bad!"

"Keep an eye out, Willy, this might be some kind of trick," Barney said. When Willy gave him a surprised look, Barney added, "It happens. You'd be amazed."

This boy looked genuine to Barney though, so he climbed down from the driver's box as the boy ran up. Closer up it was plain to see he was bleeding slightly from scratches and had torn his dusty trousers. His shirt was almost as black with soot as his face.

"What happened boy?"

"There were riders. They just started shooting everybody. They shot my pa and my brother —" The boy put his head down and Barney realized he was gasping for air. He must have run a fair distance.

"They attack the station?"

"That's what I said. They killed my pa and my brother. He runs the trading post."

"What about McGilvery the station agent?"

"They killed him and the hostler. Mrs. McGilvery too. Everyone but my ma. She made my sister and I hide in the root cellar when the shooting started. We could hear it. I came out when the shooting stopped but I made my sister stay in the cellar."

"She still there?"

"No. My ma was hurt but she was laying in the tall grass by the house. She motioned for me to get down and then put her finger to her lips. I crawled over to her and could see she was bleeding real bad. I didn't know about the others until the riders left."

"They were still there when you came out of the root cellar."

The boy nodded. "I could hear them in the trading post. They loaded everything they could on the relay horses. Got all our food for sure except what was in the root cellar. They never bothered to go in there."

"That was lucky."

"No, it wasn't," the boy said. "I couldn''t get to my rifle," he added as an afterthought. "I could have shot a couple of them, I'll bet.""

Barney contemplated the boy. Whatever tears he had shed had dried some time ago, but their tracks were visible through the soot.

The three passengers had climbed out of the coach and were listening anxiously. "Driver, you need to turn this stage around right now," said a middle-aged woman whose graying hair was pulled back in a tight bun. ""We need to get this boy to safety and ourselves as well." She walked over to the boy and put an arm around his shoulder, but he shrank away from her.

"We need to help my ma and get my sister. Ma told me to come get you because she knew there was a stage today. You've got to come help her!"

"What if the killers are still there?" said one of the two men who were passengers. He looked like a peddler to Barney, but his worn suit covered a fancy vest and Barney decided he might be a gambling man of some sort.

The other man was tall, dressed in newer clothes and had a watch on a chain. "Don't be ridiculous, Albert," he said to the first, ““the boy obviously came out after they left.”

The boy glared at Albert. “They headed west. I could see the dust.”

Barney sighed. “You said they took the relay stock?” The boy nodded. “All of the horses?””

“They even took our old mule that we used to plow with.”

Barney looked at his team. They weren’t in too bad a shape, but he knew from experience that if he headed back now, the additional miles would take their toll. If the raiders decided to double back and give chase, or if the Cheyenne he had seen were to come after them, he wouldn’t be able to run the horses very far before they would give out and then all of them could be in a worse predicament that they were now.

“Son, how bad was your mother hurt? Was she shot? Stabbed? Clubbed?”

“They shot her. She was holding her stomach. I got her a blanket and put it over her before I left because she said she was getting cold. She told Allie—that’s my sister——to go back in the root cellar and hide, but Allie never listens to anyone. She was crying anyway and holding ma’s hand. I don’t think ma minded it.”

As it stood, it was dangerous to go forward, but they might be able to help the mother and certainly could get the sister. He could also rest the horses overnight and they would be fresher for tomorrow whether they decided to push on or return to Council Grove.

CHAPTER THREE

Determination

"Driver, we're wasting time," the woman said again. "We need to get to a safe place. We're vulnerable out here in the open."

"I don't disagree with that," Barney said. He looked up. Sun Qi was standing on the roof of the coach and he was looking at the horizon before them. He looked down at Barney, and when their eyes met, Barney knew he had seen the Cheyenne heading for the smoke. "Why don't you all get inside and we'll get going again.""

"Come along, boy," the woman said. "What's your name?""

"Farrell. Farrell Gunn." He looked from the woman to Barney. "Can I ride up with you?"

"Nonsense," the woman said. "It's much too dangerous. You could fall off and break your neck."

"Madam, I think the boy could ride up with me."

"My name, sir, is Mrs. Rutledge," the woman said, "I have five grown sons and I believe I have a much better idea of what is safe for a boy than you do.""

"Long as he holds on he'll be just fine."

"And what if those outlaws have come around and are waiting for us? He will be safer inside."

Barney wanted to tell her that if any shooting started there would be little cover either way, but he held back. "They aren't likely to double back, but if they do, I need him up on top with me so that we can identify who they are.""

"I should think it would be obvious," Mrs. Rutledge said as she raised her head up and gave him a stern look. "I suspect this is not a well-traveled road. It certainly seems unkempt."

Barney shrugged. "It's traveled well enough. But with the war, folks are more cautious."

"At least we don't have any Indians to worry about," the tall passenger chimed in, and Barney could see Willy was likely to speak up. ""I think we should go forward as well. This boy has been brave to come get us on his own. That deserves a reward at least."

"Indians generally stay on the reservation now unless a few braves go out on a hunt," Barney said before Willy had a chance to speak. "I don''t worry much about that." He shot a look at Willy who covered his mouth with his hand as though he might blurt something out.

"Driver, if there is any chance of danger, I still believe Farrell—that was your name, wasn't it, young man—should ride inside with us."

Barney had decided the woman was going to pester him until she got her way, but he wanted to get going, so he reluctantly pushed the boy along and told him to climb into the coach. As soon as the passengers were settled in, he clucked the team and they started toward Diamond Springs Station again.

Barney caught Sun Qi's attention and motioned him forward. "Did you see anything?"

"Dust. Headed toward station."

"Could you make out how many?"

Sun Qi held up seven fingers. Barney had noticed that his limited English hadn't encompassed numbers yet although he seemed adept at adding up figures in Chinese.

"You're sure?"

"Maybe one more."

"That means we're outnumbered," Willy chimed in.

"Doesn't mean we're outgunned," Barney said. ""You've got the shotgun and a pistol. I've got my pistol and this rifle. I noticed the taller passenger was holstered. Most of the Cheyenne just have bows and arrows since the army took away what guns they could find.""

"I still think it would be safer to turn back."

"We have to get the boy's sister and see if we can help his mother."

"You heard what he said. She's gut shot for certain and probably has bled out by now."

Barney agreed silently, but said nothing. He was more concerned with Farrell's sister. If the Cheyenne did go to Diamond Springs and spotted her, there was a good chance they could take off with her. The Cheyenne tended to take small children captive, not kill them.

"You know Willy, it would be irresponsible for us to turn around right now," Barney said after a moment. "I can't believe you'd want to leave that little girl out there to fend for herself. Is that what you want me to do?"

"Well, now, if she goes back in the root cellar ..."

"No matter where she hides she's likely to leave tracks or sign, and Cheyenne will have no trouble reading either. How do we know she hasn't taken off after her brother? If they read her tracks and follow her, she'll lead them right to us."

"You think they saw us?"

"I'm sure of it. But if they know about the Sun brothers, it might make them cautious enough to leave well enough alone and continue their hunting. Hopefully in a different direction because the Campy boys have killed their share of Indians as well.""

Barney hurried the team along as fast as he dared without tiring them unnecessarily. He knew they would need the night to recover if he was to take the coach back in the morning, but he had already decided not to make up his mind until he actually saw the situation at Diamond Springs. They were now only a couple of miles away, but the smoke had thinned.

He hadn't seen the Cheyenne for a while, but he was busy guiding the team through a stretch of road that hugged the curves of the small hills and seldom scanned the horizon for more than a few seconds. Whoever said Kansas was flat had never driven a stagecoach, he was sure of that.

CHAPTER FOUR

Decimation

The next three miles were uneventful. Willy was quiet and appeared to concentrate on spotting hostiles of any kind. Barney could tell his team was flagging. Both his wheelers, the horses hitched closest to the stage, were pulling with droopy heads. He could feel the fatigue in the off lead. Only the near lead felt fresh on the ribbons.

The column of smoke had dwindled by the time the coach neared Diamond Springs. They could smell the fire destruction from almost a mile away. As the coach came over the last hill, Barney could see the fires were down to us smolder.

To his left, the way station had burned most of the interior, but its stone walls were only charred. Two bodies sprawled in front of the building. Across the road only the stubs of charred framing were left to show where the trading post had been. One body lay in the doorway. The fire had burned the torso and head, but the legs seemed undamaged.

Farther down the stable had only lost its roof. The walls were still intact, but charred. A body had pitched over the watering trough and another lay at the gate of the empty corral. Barney saw no sign of Farrell's mother or sister.

"Oh my God," Willy said. "They killed all of them."

Barney brought the coach to a halt. Sun Qi came across the roof, tapped him on the shoulder, and pointed at the tracks on the ground beside the coach. "Yes, I see them," Barney said.

"See what?" Willy asked.

"Two sets of tracks," Barney answered. "Some horses wearing shoes, some not. The Cheyenne have been here. I don't think they still are, or we would have been attacked. Even so, keep your eyes open."

Before Barney could climb down, the passengers started to spill out of the coach. Farrell ran behind the burnt trading post and Mrs. Rutledge trailed him as fast as her heavy skirt would allow. Barney hopped down and was close behind them. Behind the burnt building lay the body of a young man in his late teens. He had been shot four or five times. Barney figured he must be Farrell's brother.

Farrell was tearing through the tall grass, though, leaving Mrs. Rutledge farther and farther behind. The grass came almost to the boy's chest, and Barney thought there were worse places to hide. The boy stopped suddenly and disappeared from sight as he knelt down.

He popped up a moment later and waved to Barney. "She's alive! She's still alive!""

Barney passed Mrs. Rutledge as he noticed the root cellar where the boy had originally hid. It was low with a half-wall of thick turf "brick" and roofed with planks. Steps had been dug in the ground leading to a door that was below the grade level. The door was open now.

As soon as he saw her, Barney knew Farrell's mother was near the end. She had been shot in the belly, and was lying in a pool of blood that had congealed around the edge, but was fresher near the woman's body. She was trying to keep her eyes open, but the lids kept falling. Her mouth moved as though trying to form words, but when Barney bent close, he could only make out the word "taken."

"The outlaws took my sister," Farrell said.

"We don't know that yet," Barney replied as he looked around. "She''d be hard to find in this grass, and I didn't see any sign that the grass had been disturbed except for where you were running. And of course her." He pointed to Mrs. Rutledge as she reached them. ""Naturally, with that broad skirt, we won't be able to tell now," he added with annoyance.

Looking at the grass around Farrell's mother, though, Barney thought it unlikely that the Cheyenne had found her or even realized she was here.

Farrell was stroking her head, and she was trying to form another word. "She says they took Allie," he said and looked up at Barney. "I should have stayed here. I should have protected her."

Barney shook his head. "They would have taken you too. Don't believe you could have stopped them."

Mrs. Rutledge kneeled down beside the boy. "Don't worry, ma'am. I'll see your son is taken care of."

Farrell's mother didn't reply, but closed her eyes. A moment later, a brief shudder told Barney that she had passed to the other side.

CHAPTER FIVE

Decision

Barney left the boy with his mother and Mrs. Rutledge. The two passengers had followed them, but had stopped at the edge of the grassy field. Barney asked them to see if they could find a shovel or something to dig with. He knew they might not be able to dig graves for everyone, but he was determined to do something with the bodies to prevent wild animals from getting to them.

Sun Qi had already begun to unharness the stock, but Barney stopped him. "I need you to do something for me," he said. "You have some tracking skills. I need you to look around and see if you can figure out where the Cheyenne went and where the raiders went."

"White men went on down road. Easy to see the prints."

“I figured the same. Question is: How far?”

“Took other horse. All food supplies.”

“Think they will head for the next way station.”

Sun Qi shook his head. “Go far now. Too much supply slow down.”

“Not if that’s what they’re looking for. Quantrill might have sent them out to gather supplies. In any case, they won’t be coming back here tonight, but I’d feel better if I knew where the Indians went. Okay? But I want you back by sunset. And don’t get yourself killed.”

Sun Qi nodded. “Not my time.”

“Make sure it isn’t. Get started, it’s getting late in the day. I’ll get Willy to help me with the horses. ”

With the help of the two passengers and Willy, Barney moved the McGilverys and the two dead hostlers away from the road and found a spot where a natural indentation allowed them to get the bodies covered quickly with brush.

The two passengers, whose name he remembered as Hoffer and Wilkes, had found a shovel, but balked at the idea of digging graves. “I feel bad for these folks, of course, but digging seven graves is going to take longer than we have to spare,” said Wilkes, the taller passenger who had remained holstered during the trip. The smaller man, Hoffer, had dug through his luggage and found an old Volcanic pistol that Barney was sure would only be accurate to a few feet but would stop an angry body in its tracks.

As a compromise, he had them dig a shallow grave for Farrell's mother, and while they worked on that, he enlisted Willy to help him move Farrell's father and brother behind the destroyed trading post. The two of them covered the bodies with rock, and Farrell came up to help them.

Barney was worried about the boy. He moved rock and looked at the bodies without any sign of emotion. Barney had seen folks react all sorts of ways to death, but he always found the dull face of unspeakable pain to be the worst.

The peddler, Hoffer, had a small canvas tarp in his luggage, so they used that as a shroud for Mrs. Gunn and buried her in the only grave that had gotten dug. Barney knew the hole was probably too shallow, but had better sense than to say anything.

Mrs. Rutledge, however, had no problem speaking her mind and Hoffer and Wilkes found themselves digging it deeper than they had originally planned, although Willy now took a turn. After the woman was lowered down, Mrs. Rutledge said a few words over her and prodded Farrell to say something, but he remained silent, just standing stiffly until the men finished shoveling dirt into the grave.

Barney built a fire up against the rock wall of the destroyed station. He hoped if either the renegades or the marauders saw the smoke, they would just figure it was a flash start from the fires that had already burned.

Sun Qi came back as the sun was going down. He confirmed there were seven warriors on horses, but they had split up. Two had headed to the southeast, but the other five had turned to the northeast. He did not think they would be coming back this way.

"Do you think they are headed for Council Grove?" Willy asked.

"That wouldn't make much sense," Barney said. "They''ve already seen us and know we're west of them now. If they wanted to attack, they could have just waited for us here." Truth be told, Barney thought to himself, it didn't make any sense to him that they hadn't been attacked. He had been waiting for it most of the afternoon.

What little food was on the stage was shared with all the passengers and Farrell. The boy seemed oblivious to his surroundings now and just sat and looked into the fire. Mrs. Rutledge tried to talk to him, but he ignored her. Barney sat down next to him, though, and the boy leaned against him.

"Put your arm around him and comfort him," Mrs. Rutledge said.

"He don't want that," Barney answered. "He just wants to lean on me while he thinks his thoughts. That so boy?" Farrell nodded once but didn't speak.

After a while, Barney realized the boy had fallen asleep. He lifted him carefully and carried him to the coach. Sun Qi opened the door and Barney climbed in and positioned the boy so he was sleeping on the thin cushions of the passenger seats.

"The boy seems to trust you," Mrs. Rutledge observed when Barney came back to the fire.

"Misplaced faith," Barney answered. "We all have it in some form or other."

"You're not a trustworthy man?"

"No, I'm trustworthy in my own realm. I'm no parent, though, and that's what the boy could use right now."

"He's thinking about his sister, you know."

"Yes, in the space of a day he's lost everyone he's ever loved. That's hard on a man, let alone a boy."

"When we get to the end of our journey, I will see that he is taken care of," Mrs. Rutledge said. "I am going all the way to Santa Fe. My son has a ranch near there, and I''m sure he will take the boy in."

"He might have kinfolk somewhere that would want him."

"If I can find them, I will. He mentioned an aunt, perhaps in Massachusetts or Rhode Island. He doesn't remember her name, though, and has never seen her. His mother just referred to her as Elizabeth."

"Might be hard to find."

"I'll make the effort once we get to Santa Fe." She raised an eyebrow, "We are going west, I presume."

Barney hesitated, "Yes. Well. About that...."

CHAPTER SIX

Darkness

Sundown lingered on the western horizon. Sun Qi had decided to follow the tracks of the raiders as far as he could. The boy and the passengers sat by the fire, along with Willy who was entertaining them with a tale of his childhood exploit that resulted in a leg so poorly set it was keeping him out of the military.

Barney wandered around the compound, but kept his eyes to the east. He wasn't convinced the Cheyenne wouldn't double back. He reckoned the evening would be chilly in spite of the gentle late summer heat, but he had decided to douse the fire as soon as the sun dipped below half on the horizon. No point in making them too easy to find in the darkness, even though Sun Qi would need to find them too.

He never worried about the Chinaman, though. The man could see in the dark. They had been together now for a few years and Sun had always held up his end of the partnership and then some. Barney had saved him from being beaten to death by a bunch of drunk cowhands one fateful November night. Sun had declared his eternal gratefulness and explained that it was his duty to return the favor. As far as Barney was concerned, Sun had returned it now several times over, but Sun didn't see it that way.

The two of them had slipped into a strange friendship, Barney thought as he scanned the eastern rise for any sign of movement. Sun Qi always surprised him with the depth of his practical knowledge. He was a better tracker than Barney for sure, and when Barney had asked him how he had come upon such knowledge, Sun Qi had told him of a boyhood spent in warfare in a distant land.

The Chinaman had come to America to work on the railroads and to get away from the fighting, but soon discovered an enemy in the camp and had to flee. Barney was surprised to find that the Chinese had their disputes like everyone else, and Sun Qi's life was in danger to stay. When Barney pressed him, he wouldn''t discuss the reason for dispute except to say he was once an honored guard of an important person who was overthrown. That person's enemies also had sent people to America to make sure no one who had escaped would return to China.

Amazingly Sun had worked his way east across the country, mostly on foot, at a time where everyone else was heading west. Barney knew the man was as tough as anyone he had ever met even though he couldn't fire a gun and could barely stay on a horse. In fact, Sun Qi reminded him of an Indian scout more than a coolie. He certainly could track like an Indian, and his patience and ability to move silently or remain in one position for hours was beyond anyone in Barney's experience.

Barney decided it was time to put out the fire. He took one last look to the ridge and walked back to the small camp by the station. The passengers made no objection when he explained that the light would be a beacon if anyone was intent on doing them harm.

"You think the outlaws will come back?" the short passenger, Hoffer, asked him.

"Hope not, but I think it would be foolish not to plan for it." Barney would have liked to hide everyone in the ruin of the station, but what was left of its floor was still smoldering although no flame had shown for an hour. Better to camp against the exterior wall and then run inside for protection if they were attacked.

He shared his thought with the passengers, but Mrs. Rutledge said she would prefer to try sleeping in the coach. "I'm afraid that my constitution is not up to a night under the stars,"" she said firmly. "The boy should stay in there as well."

"If we have to make a stand from attack, our best position is inside the station behind what's left of the walls," Barney explained. ""If you stay inside the coach, you won't be able to run in there quickly."

"If we're attacked, I seriously doubt we will be able to do much about it," she said. "You men might think you can defend yourselves, but I very much fear the best bet for the boy and I would be to hide now. Yet there is no place to hide, therefore, we might as well be comfortable." She lifted her chin as she said the last words, and Barney knew he was not going to be able to persuade her otherwise.

"Why don't you go ahead and sleep in the coach," he said as he wondered how he could find some advantage in the situation. ""Willy, why don't you keep watch on the roof and then you could give her some covering fire if need be. That's about the highest ground around short of climbing this cottonwood.""

"On top of the coach?" Willy asked. "Which way am I keeping watch?"

"You keep an eye on that ridge to the east. I'll keep an eye to the west. Maybe Mr. Hoffer and Mr. Wilkes can spell us a bit during the night."

"Where's the Chinaman? Has he run off?" Wilkes said.

"I asked him to scout a ways west. I want to know where those raiders went. If they didn't have any qualms about killing the folks here, well ..." He could see by their faces he didn't need to finish his sentence.

"I don't want to die," Hoffer said in a small voice. "Not out here."

"That's why we're being cautious, sir," Barney said with as much hopefulness in his voice as he could muster. "None of us want anything to happen, so we're just going to do a few reasonable things to keep ourselves alive and kicking."

He spotted movement along the road to the west and raised his rifle. The others followed his gaze, but even in the remaining light of dusk it was plain the figure walking toward them with raised hands was Sun Qi.

His report was brief. He had walked about three miles and had spotted campfires about six to eight miles farther on. Unless some group they didn't know about was in the area, the raiders had not gone very far after leaving Diamond Springs. Barney was glad he had put out the fire. If the raiders sent out their own patrol, it would be unlikely they would come back as far as the station, but might go far enough to see a fire.

"Well folks, all we can do now is get a good night's sleep, or at least as good as we can."

"What about tomorrow?" Mrs. Rutledge said.

"Tomorrow we'll have to decide which way to go. But let's sleep on it while we have the chance."

CHAPTER SEVEN

Designs

Everyone had bedded down as well as they could. Barney allowed himself to lean up against the wall and fell asleep knowing that Sun would be keeping a watch whether anyone else fell asleep. He often wondered at the Chinaman's ability to remain calm in any kind of crisis. Sun had tried to teach him to meditate as he could, but Barney had never been able to empty his mind for more than a few seconds or to master how you could be totally aware yet have an empty mind. Seemed like a lot of hokum, but he had seen how Sun managed to sleep, but not sleep, think, but not think, and he was jealous of that ability.

He woke up to a small voice whispering in his ear. "Mr. Driver, are you awake," the boy said.

"Why aren't you in the wagon?"

"Mrs. Rutledge snores. And I couldn't sleep. I was afraid I might start dreaming."

"Afraid of dreaming? Dreams won't hurt you none."

"What if I dream about today? I can't stop thinking about it."

No, Barney thought, you never will. "Go back and try to get some rest, boy. Tomorrow could be a busy day."

"Farrell. My name is Farrell. Pa called me Farr."

"Farr, you go on back in the coach and try to rest."

"Can't. I'm scared. And she's snoring loud.""

"Then lay down on the ground here. You can have my coverlet."

The half-moon was bright overhead and Barney found he could see clearly in its light. He wished it were darker. If anyone was watching, they would have seen the boy coming from the coach to the wall.

The boy took his coverlet, but instead of laying on the ground, he sat cross-legged next to Barney and rested his back against the wall as well. "Mrs. Rutledge plans to take me with her," he said in a small voice.

"Best thing. She'll help you find your aunt maybe, or give you a home. At least you'll have someone to take care of you.""

"I don't want to go with her."

"Not much choice."

"Could I stay with you? And your Chinaman?"

"Why would you want to do that?"

"Don't want to go with Mrs. Rutledge. She seems mean. Bossy."

"Yeah, well, I'm always on the road and Sun goes with me."

"I could sit with him. While we're on the road, I mean." The boy leaned back against the wall. "I don't want to sleep."

"I do," Barney said and closed his eyes. He waited for what seemed like five minutes before he Indian a look at the boy. He was still watching Barney." You can''t come with me and Sun. If you don't want to go with Mrs. Rutledge, that's fine. We'll see if we can find someone in Council Grove to take care of you."

"Is that where you live? Council Grove?"

"When I live anywhere. Mostly I just live on the stage and sleep in a hotel between runs."

"I could learn to do that. Drive a stage. I could already drive our wagon."

"What, one mule?"

"Yes, but Pa let me drive it."

"A stage is different. You have the horses to worry about, but you also have the people you are carrying and they are a much bigger worry, I'll tell you." He was worrying about them now. Even from where he sat he could tell that Willy was already asleep on the top of the coach. He had told Willy specifically to keep watch. If he didn't think they needed to keep quiet, he would have gone over right now and roused him with a few hot words. But they would keep until sunrise.

"I could handle it. I want to learn."

"Why?"

"Because then I can stay here and find the men."

"What men?"

"The ones that killed my family. I'm going to find them someday. Then I'm going to kill them." Barney was chilled by the conviction in the little voice.

"I understand that you want to do that, son. Only natural. But don't start dwelling on it just yet. Sun Qi tells me the best way to accomplish something is not to want it."

"What does that mean?"

"You'll have to ask him. I don't understand it myself. But it seems to keep him sensible."

"Why did they kill my folks? They could have took everything we had and not killed them. Or the McGilverys. Or Teddie and Richard. Why did they have to kill everyone?"

Barney shook his head. "Makes no sense to me, boy. Just plain hateful."

"Then they don't deserve to live."

Barney looked at the somber face in the moonlight. "Everyone deserves to live, boy. Everything has its time. Grass. Trees. Cows. Horses. Even nasty critters like snakes and wolves. But when the time is up, it's just up. That''s all there is to that."

The boy looked puzzled. "I don't understand what you mean?"

"Not sure myself. Just that, maybe that it's okay to seek justice, even retribution, but not if it makes you just as bad as the outlaw. That make sense?"

The boy nodded. "I'll think on it."

"You do that. I'll bet your ma and pa would tell you the same."

The boy closed his eyes and leaned back against the wall again. "They ain't here anymore."

CHAPTER EIGHT

Daybreak

At daybreak Barney gathered everyone and told them after a hard night of thinking, he had decided they would head back to Council Grove.

“That’s ridiculous,” Mrs. Rutledge said almost before he had finished. “We know the Indians are in that direction.”

“Yes, ma’am, but we also know that the men who killed all these folks are only about nine or ten miles to the west of us.”

“Then we should just stay put for another day and push on.” Barney noticed that Hoffer and Wilkes were nodding agreement. Willy didn’t seem to be paying any attention to the gathering argument.

“We could do that, but then there is still the chance the Indians will circle back here if they don't see the coach. We're sure they saw us out on the road before they came here. Maybe they just cleared out so there wouldn't be a confrontation."

"That doesn't make sense from all I've heard about Indians," Wilkes spoke up. "Besides, we know they took the girl." He looked down not wanting to meet Farrell's gaze. "Why would they take her if they knew we were coming?"

"You can't paint all the Cheyenne with one brush," Barney said. "For all we know they took her to make sure she was safe."

"You don't believe that."

"I don't know because I don't know if that is a war party or a hunting party. If it's just a hunting party, they may have taken her along for safekeeping while they range for game."

"How can we know?" Mrs. Rutledge asked.

"I think the best thing to do is to go ahead a couple of miles and then let Sun Qi hop down and get ahead of us. The horses normally get a day's rest in between runs, so they are likely still a little tired. Good for them if we take it slow at first."" Especially if we have to make a run for it, he thought to himself. "If we let him get well ahead, he can give us any warning if there's a chance of attack."

"But he will be on foot and they will be mounted," Wilkes said. "He's a Chinaman. For all we know he'll run and hide if he sees them."

Barney frowned at the man. "I've known him for a long time, and he's never run from trouble. I trust him a sight more than I do you, sir."

"Wilkes is right, though," Hoffer jumped in. "The Chinaman will be on foot and the Indians are mounted. They could ride him down before he could have time to warn us. I''d just as soon stay here."

Willy stepped closer and towered over Hoffer. "Listen folks, Barney here has got more experience than any other driver on this line. If he says our best play is to go, then that's all there is to it."" He looked hard at Wilkes and Hoffer. "You forget that we have our guns. As far as we know, the Indians don't. The army took them away from what I've heard. If they have any sense, they'll leave us alone. That's the long and short of it, we either head toward men who have guns and use them or we leave them as far behind as we can."

Barney was surprised that Willy had cut to the bone of the argument. Wilkes and Hoffer shuffled their feet but didn't respond. Mrs. Wilkes drew herself up and said, "Very well then. We should accede to Mr. Todd''s direction. How soon do you plan to leave?"

"We should head out as soon as the horses are hitched. If any of you need to relieve yourselves, Indian the time to do it."

Hoffer looked around at everyone and hurried beyond the charred station toward a small stand of trees in back of it. The others moved off to the stage. Mrs. Rutledge had Farrell in hand. Although he looked back at Barney, he didn't argue when she told him to climb in the coach.

By the time Hoffer was done, Sun Qi had finished hitching the team. With Hoffer aboard, Barney climbed up to the box and Willy came up the other side. Sun Qi took his normal spot at the rear of the roof.

Barney leaned toward Willy, "Thanks for that. They needed that extra persuading."

Willy shrugged. "I'm not worried. Might want to let me have that rifle, though. If we see them I could fire a shot over their head to let them know we don't want company."

"I'll give you the rifle, but don't shoot at anything unless I give you the word," Barney said. "Probably not a good idea to go shooting at them unless they look like they are going to come at us. Might make them more angry than fearful, and we don't want that."

"You're the boss."

Whether I want to be or not, Barney thought as he flicked the reins to start the team moving.

CHAPTER NINE

Disquiet

The early sun promised a hot, bright day, and already the horizon ahead shimmered as a gentle breeze lilted along the tall grass. Barney kept the pace slow. The team seemed rested, but the near lead wasn't moving with his usual bounce, so Barney knew that he was still a little tired from yesterday''s run.

For once Willy seemed alert to the surroundings and Barney noticed that he kept looking around to see if he could spot anything. If he could at least learn to stay alert, Willy might become a decent shotgun messenger. There was more to the job than carrying a shotgun. Although he hadn't said anything to the passengers, Barney knew that the strongbox he had under a coverlet between him and Willy probably contained either cash for one of the banks down in Wichita or pay for the soldiers at Fort Larned.

As planned, Barney went just a couple of miles before halting his team and beckoning to Sun Qi. When he outlined what he thought needed to be done, he was surprised when Sun Qi disagreed.

"I know you're not afraid, so what's the problem?"

"Not fast like arrow. In the open, either hide or run. Hide is best. How warn you then?"

"You don't think you could spot them before they see you?"

Sun Qi shrugged. "Easier to see from up here."

"What if you just get a mile or so ahead of us and stay near the road? Then we could just pick you up as we get there."

Sun Qi shook his head again. "If I signal, you not have time to pick me up. How you turn?"

Barney knew Sun was right. Although a few places were suitable for turning the coach, this particular road had been used enough that a slight bank had formed on the sides, and most of way the road crested the low hills. Although not steep, once you began turning you risked tipping the coach unless you took the turn dangerously slow.

“So you think we just push on?”

“Push on. Be ready. I keep watch behind. Willy, you watch ahead.”

Wilkes had stuck his head out of the coach to ask what was wrong. Barney passed the reins to Sun and jumped down to explain the change in plans.

“I told you not to count on the Chinaman,” Wilkes said.

“I do count on him, Mr. Wilkes, and he’s right. He’d never make it back to us in time. Getting back to Council Grove is still our best option.””

“We’re going so slow,” Hoffer said. “I can feel every bump.””

“We’re going to keep a slower pace. The horses are still tired, but Council Grove isn’t all that far. We should still be able to reach it by early afternoon.””

“Then what?” Wilkes asked. “The raiders will still be in front of us.”

“Then we let the army know what has happened and I’m sure we will get an escort at least to Henderson’s station, the one beyond Diamond Springs, and they can get a patrol to go look for Farrell’s sister.” In his mind, though, he wondered if the raiders were hitting that station even now.

"In that case, please climb back up and let's get going again, Mr. Todd," said Mrs. Rutledge from her seat in the opposite corner. ""The sun is climbing and it is likely to become unpleasantly warm before we reach town. Let's not prolong our duress any more than necessary."

Barney nodded to her. "Just so, ma'am. Haven't seen any sign of trouble yet. You men keep your pistols handy, though, just in case." He climbed back up the front wheel to the driver's box. He had noticed the boy was sitting oddly quiet. Hadn't even made his usual plea to sit on top.

In spite of what he had told the boy last night, Barney was almost certain the girl was headed back to Cheyenne country as a prisoner to be given to some squaw as a prize. The certainty had grown since Sun Qi told him the party had split up, especially since just two had turned toward the reservation.

The rumor going round was that the Confederacy was going to enlist the Cheyenne and Kiowa to fight the soldiers stationed in Kansas. Barney didn't believe that for a moment, but people always liked to talk. If they were recruiting, though, they might also be providing some rifles and ammunition. That situation concerned him the most.

CHAPTER TEN

Delay

The next three miles were uneventful as Barney suspected they would be. On both sides of the road the terrain had gentle slopes that would make it hard for anyone on horseback to hide. As he began to feel the road rise, though, Barney decided to stop once again. They had reached the start of 10-Mile Hill and he knew the horses would be straining more as they pulled up its reasonably easy lower slope. As the road reached the peak of the hill though, the slope became much greater, and boulders near the top made it necessary to take a sharp turn at the peak before heading downhill again.

Worse, the terrain near the peak was undulating, providing small pockets between the ridges where it would be no problem for two or three riders to hide unseen. But it was the boulders at the peak which gave him the most concern. If there was going to be an ambush, he was certain that's where it would happen.

When Wilkes called out to him again, he explained why he had stopped without bothering to climb down from the box. The boy's voice came up to him, asking if he could ride up with Barney, but Barney told him to stay in the coach with Mrs. Rutledge.

With a flick of his wrist the team began the slow climb. Barney wondered if he had made the right choice. Perhaps they could have stayed at the station. Even in ruins the station house provided some cover. On the other hand, it was much harder to shoot at an object in motion, especially with a bow and arrow, so he reasoned to himself that the stage still gave them the best chance of survival.

The worst spot would be the last pull to the top. The grade was steeper there although the height of the coach box would give them an advantage if they had to fire their weapons. Barney had mastered the art of holding one set of reins in his teeth while he fired a pistol with his free hand. It was a skill you developed from having a long career as a whip, and if you didn't develop it, you likely wouldn't have a long career.

Trouble was, it was a skill you could only use on straight stretches. He'd have to have the ribbons in both hands once they topped the hill and made the turn to the left. It was up to the near lead at that point, and Barney wished he had thought about putting his steadier lead in that spot, but it was too late now. He was confident of the two wheelers, but the new boy would have to show his mettle or they could be in a spot of trouble.

"I don't see anything yet," Willy said from his seat.

"Keep a good eye. If they come, I expect them to come from my right," Barney replied. "They'll figure I'm too busy to shoot at them."

"Can your Chinaman use a gun?"

"Couldn't hit a feed sack in a grain mill. I've tried to teach him. He gets the notion, but can't seem to hold steady once he pulls the trigger." Barney had tried to teach Sun how to use a rifle a couple of times, but the Chinaman shied whenever he fired the weapon. On the other hand, he was dead clean with a bow which seemed to be his choice of weapon for hunting. For a hand fight, Sun was hell on wheels in a close combat. Barney had never seen anything like him before——all kicks and spins and short punches that usually brought an opponent down in moments, sometimes permanently. Sun had tried to show Barney, but he just wasn't flexible enough to get the movements. So they balanced out in some odd sort of way, he thought.

"What's he gonna do if they attack? He's just sitting back there."

"He'll figure something out," Barney said. "Always does. He''s as dangerous as they come."

"If I have to shoot behind us, he'd better duck."

"He will, but don't be shooting him on accident. He'll figure out some way to help out. You can count on it."

Barney glanced over. Willy looked like he didn't believe what Barney was telling him, but shrugged. "We'll see. Think our passengers can shoot?"

"I'd bet on Wilkes but not the other one. He's a peddler of some kind and I don't imagine he's had much practice with that little pea shooter of his."

Ahead Barney could see the road rising more steeply. He decided their best move was to drive up the hill as fast as possible. If they were going to be ambushed, there was nowhere to turn around here. The best play was to get through that turn as fast as possible. Once they were on the downhill side, they had a fighting chance to make a run for it.

Great idea, he thought, but nothing is ever that easy. If the Cheyenne only had their hunting bows, then running the team might discourage them. If they had a rifle or two, it might be another story.

He flicked the ribbons again to urge the team up. He could feel they were a little tired, but not spent. They would make the peak with some speed, and if they topped it safely, he would run them a half mile more and then slow down. He didn't think the Indians would attack once he was far enough along the downhill slope. Then it would be easier to get the team up to speed, but more than that, he doubted the renegades would want to get that close to Council Grove where soldiers often patrolled.

The near lead was putting his ears back a little, making Barney wonder if he was asking too much from the team. He didn't wonder long. Behind him Sun Qi shouted.

"They come."

CHAPTER ELEVEN

Deception

Barney chanced a quick look back. Two mounted braves were galloping out from behind a hillock to his right as he'd predicted.

One of them had a rifle.

As the brave brought it up, Barney yelled for everyone to duck. An angry bee buzzed past him just below his knee but above the level of the team. He slapped the reins again and both leads put their ears back. Even when they had rifles, most Indians seldom had more than a few bullets. Barney figured they weren't likely to take many shots until they could get a good bead. If he could move the stage fast enough, the one with the rifle might think twice about firing again.

"They're coming up fast," Willy yelled and fired a shot with the rifle. "Damn. Missed. Just two of them. Must be the two that broke off from the others. One's coming up your side, Barney."

The slope was straight. Barney put the off reins in his left hand, pulled his pistol, and risked a quick glance back. The one with the rifle was coming up fast, but Barney wanted him closer. He couldn't see the other brave.

"Damn. Shit. Oh hell," Willy yelled and fired the rifle. Barney looked over to see an arrow had caught Willy just under his shoulder, maybe in the armpit. The arrow had gone through his coat and was sticking out the back at an odd angle. If there hadn''t been blood, Barney would have thought it had only gone through the coat.

"Is it bad," Barney called.

"No, just hurts like hell. I can still shoot and I'm gonna shoot that bastard right now."

Barney looked back in time to see the brave coming up almost within range. He fired in the general direction of the horse and was rewarded by a spurt of blood from its shoulder. The pony jolted to a stop as the brave brought his rifle up to fire. When he did, the angle of the rifle changed and the shot went into the road behind the coach wheels.

He holstered his pistol because the turn was coming up. He heard Willy fire again and curse. "Aim for the horse," Barney hollered.

"Can't aim for anything bouncing like this. Look out!"

An arrow zinged past Barney's face. Close but not too close.

All four of his team had their ears back now. He could feel them tiring through the reins, but knew there was enough left in them to do what he needed them to do.

Scanning quickly, he saw no sign of the other warriors. He hoped Willy was right that just the two had pursued them. But there were plenty of places to hide among the boulders ahead.

As though the team could sense the top, they gave just a little surge the made Barney thrill in his fingers. Another shot went overhead. The brave must have dismounted and now had a better chance for a good shot by shooting from a firm base. Barney was more worried about Sun than himself because now he was protected by the coach behind him. He hoped the baggage would stop any low shot because a bullet could pierce through the boot to the inside of the coach. It had happened before. He yelled for the passengers to get down inside, but doubted they could hear him over the rattle of the trees and wheels and the coach itself.

Just as they topped the hill and Barney began to turn his near lead to the left, a rifle shot came from that side. He felt the near lead stumble even as he tried to turn on Barney's command.

The horse took two more steps and went to his knees. The near wheeler piled into him and Barney felt the coach tipping to the right in the direction of the downslope. "Jump!" he hollered to Willy and let go of the reins to do that himself as the wheelers tripped over the fallen lead and the coach went slowly over on its side.

CHAPTER TWELVE

Defense

Barney hit the ground rolling, but his right shoulder was on fire and his ears were ringing. Sun Qi had landed safely and the thought that the Chinaman must be a cat whizzed through Barney's mind. Sun had his knife out of his boot, though, and was running to cut the team free from the singletree. Barney looked around for Willy, but he was splayed out at an odd angle with his chest down and a small boulder holding his face to his chest. The angle of his neck told Barney that Willy's neck was broken and he was probably dead.

He could hear a scream from inside the coach, but as he started toward it, a brave came riding straight toward Sun. The warrior had a rifle up and fired, but Sun turned and the bullet missed. Barney felt his pistol in his hand

and up and firing without even realizing he had drawn. The brave pitched over the back of his horse and didn't look like he would get up.

As he ran up from his hiding place, a second brave fired an arrow at Sun and missed. The two were now engaged in a deadly hand-to-hand that Barney had no time to watch because yet another had come from the left and was picking up the fallen rifle. He raised it and fired as Barney fired his pistol.

A strip of fire seared Barney's left bicep. Barney fired again but the brave didn't go down. He had brought the rifle up again to shoot, but it wouldn't fire. Empty, Barney thought and raised his pistol to take careful aim. Down the length of his barrel he could see the brave glaring at him defiantly. He squeezed the trigger, but the hammer clicked down on an empty chamber. He squeezed again but had the same result. Beyond the barrel he could see recognition on the brave's face.

The Indian dropped the rifle, pulled out his hunting knife, and charged Barney. Barney feinted left and moved right, the warrior's sharp blade just missing him. Barney hit the man with his pistol barrel with all the strength he had left.

The brave staggered, but didn't go down. This time he circled Barney warily. As they danced in a circle, Barney spotted Willy's pistol laying on the ground nearby. Instead of continuing his circle to the right, Barney jumped left so that the warrior wouldn't turn and see it as well. He knew he had to keep him turned until he had a chance to maneuver over toward Willy.

Sun was in a similar dance with his opponent. Both had their knives out and neither seemed in a hurry to rush the other. None of the passengers were trying to climb out of the coach, but Barney could hear someone still screaming inside.

As he moved the brave where he wanted him, Barney wondered where the other warriors were when the brave that had chased them rode up. He leaped from his horse onto the side of the carriage—now the roof. Bow in hand, he fired into the coach and was rewarded with another scream.

Barney knew he couldn't wait any longer. He dove over Willy and grabbed desperately at the pistol. Somehow he managed to find it with his hand. Later on he would think it Providence or sheer luck, but today he just rolled and, when he came up, squeezed off a shot just as the brave was charging him again. It was Providence again that guided the bullet into the man's throat, shattering the artery there and spraying blood behind.

But the shot didn't stop the follow-through and Barney felt the knife plunge high into his left shoulder but just below his collarbone. The Indian sagged against him as well, though still barely alive, but with no strength left to fight. Barney rolled the man off of him.

The Indian on the coach was pulling another arrow back when a shot from inside took him under the jaw and sent him tumbling backwards off the coach.

As he did, Sun finally managed to gain the advantage with his foe and thrust his own knife deep under the man's ribs. The warrior slumped immediately and Barney figured Sun must have tipped his heart.

As Barney stood up he could see the brave he had unhorsed earlier running toward him. Barney looked around and found the unused shotgun that had been thrown from the boot. He picked it up, but found that his left arm wouldn't help hold it, so he clapped it to his side with his right and pointed it in the general direction of the oncoming warrior.

The brave stopped. He was still too far away for the shotgun to be effective, so Barney waited. The brave gauged the scene, and with a glance at Barney, turned his back to catch one of the loose ponies. He jumped aboard, and with a last cold look at Barney, kicked the pony and rode away.

CHAPTER THIRTEEN

Deliverance

Barney could hear a strange gasping sound coming from inside the stage. He handed the shotgun to Sun Qi. "Here. That Indian comes back, wait till he's close enough then shoot him. Even you couldn''t miss at close range with this thing."

Although he shoulder burned like nothing he could remember, he found a way to pull himself up on top of the overturned stage. What he saw when he looked down into the coach made him catch his breath.

Hoffer had obviously hit the roof or the opposite side and been knocked out when the coach overturned. For a second Barney wasn't even sure he was still breathing.

Wilkes hadn't been so lucky. From the look of it, the door had open as the coach fell and

Wilkes had fallen half out, chest and head forward. The door frame sat on his chest. Barney felt tempted to jump off the top so his weight wouldn't add to the problem, but Farrell had seen where he was looking and said, "He's dead. Can you help Mrs. Rutledge?"

Farrell was holding Hoffer's little pistol in his right hand, but his left was supporting Mrs. Rutledge's head. An arrow was sticking straight out from her bosom, and from the flecking of blood coming from her lips as she tried to breathe, Barney was certain her lung had been pierced. The arrow had gone deep, and even if Barney thought he might get it out, he knew it wouldn't be of any use to her. He shook his head at Farrell.

"You got to do something," the boy cried and tears ran down his face.

"Nothing we can do. She only has a little time left. Hold her head like you're doing."

Farrell pointed the gun at him. "I said do something." His eyes had tears, but Barney could see he meant what he said.

With his bad arm, Barney lifted the top door until it was fully opened. "I'm coming down, but there ain't anything I can do. He managed to get his legs through the door and hung there for a second. His entire side burned like fire now and he wondered if it would ever stop.

Farrell managed to help guide his legs until he was able to drop inside without stepping on Mrs. Rutledge or Hoffer, but to do so he had to step on Wilkes and the knowledge of what he was doing made him shiver.

Mrs. Rutledge had turned her face to him. Her eyes were getting glassy, but she whispered something and Barney put his ear as close as he could to hear, "Take care of the boy."

He told her he would. So close to her, he could see that blood was pooling beneath her. From such a short range, it must have gone through. He heard a rasping sound he had sometimes heard before, and when he looked back at her eyes, they no longer could see anything.

"Sorry boy, she's gone," he said. "Nothing I could do.""

"I know. I could tell she was bad off. I just ... wanted to help her."

Barney turned to Hoffer. He pushed up an eyelid, but Hoffer's eyes were rolled up in his head. "Guess we ought to figure out how to get him out of here," he said.

"You're hurt," Farrell said as though he had just realized the blood down Barney's side was not someone else's.

"Don't matter, I'll live. Help me shift Mr. Hoffer here so he can be more comfortable until we figure out how to get him up out of here."" He saw Farrell was still holding the gun. "Might want to put that down so it doesn't go off while we shift him."

The boy looked at the gun as though it was a strange object someone had put in his hand. "I had to shoot that Indian. I didn't want to."

"I know. Put the gun down for now and help me."

Hoffer was lying with his back against the roof and his legs against back of the front bulkhead. With Farrell's help, Barney managed to turn the man enough to lay him straight. "We''ll figure something out when he comes to," Barney said. He wanted to get out of the coach and see if there was a coverlet or a blanket in the boot. At least something to cover the dead for now.

He heard Sun yelling for him. Barney scrambled up and managed to get his head and shoulders through the doorway, but he had to tell Farrell to help give him a push. He thought maybe they were going to be attacked again, but as he wormed his way back on top, he saw Sun pointing toward Council Grove.

"Soldiers come."

A cloud of dust was visible about three or four miles away. "How do you know they are soldiers?"

"Who else?"

"Probably so. Might have heard the shooting, but that's a long ways away." He motioned to Sun Qi to climb up on the coach with him. ""I need some help getting the boy out. Any sign of that Indian?"

Sun shook his head and handed the shotgun up to Barney. "Just boy?" he asked as he climbed up the traces on the undercarriage.

"Hoffer's hurt, but we've got to figure out how to move him. Mrs. Rutledge and Mr. Wilkes are dead."

Sun reached the top and looked in. He reached down to Farrell and said, "Take arm." When he had a firm grasp on the boy, he pulled him up through the door until the boy could catch hold and finish. The strength of Sun always surprised Barney, but he was grateful that he hadn't needed to do it.

"Farrell, could you climb down and look in the boot to see if we have anything to cover Mrs. Rutledge and Mr. Wilkes?" When the boy had clambered down the traces, Barney told Sun what the woman had asked of him.

"What do you think?" Barney finished.

"We take. I teach boy."

"Sure you can help me out on this? Never had this kind of responsibility before."

Sun Qi looked at Barney without expression. "Boy ask you. Woman ask you. Have you fear?"

Barney took a deep breath. "Damn right. I've never been a papa before."

"Don't worry. I help." For the first time ever, Barney saw the hint of a smile on the Chinaman's face. "I teach both of you."

ABOUT THE AUTHOR

A former magazine and newspaper editor, Kendall Hanson is a graduate of the University of New Mexico where he worked with and was influenced by such publishing stars as Tony Hillerman, Rudy Anaya, and Jack D Rittenhouse.

After leaving McGraw-Hill in 1998, he formed his own publishing company that focused on reprints of classic maritime and non-fiction adventure books. In 2000 he became managing editor and partner in a local newspaper which motivated him to move to the beautiful Kitsap Peninsula across the Puget Sound from Seattle.

He has owned and worked in a variety of industries from retail to insurance to financial services, but is now concentrating his efforts on the fiction career he has put off for too long.

For updates about current and upcoming releases, as well as exclusive promotions, visit the author's website at www.kdhwriter.us.

50024418R00047

Made in the USA
Lexington, KY
29 February 2016